Scientists,
Psychics
& Psychotics

A Collection of Short Stories

Neal McNeil

Copyright © 2009 by Neal McNeil

All rights reserved.

For more information contact nlmbooks@gmail.com.

To my friend, my Muse - my wife.

Contents

The EDISON Project

11:30 AM

Dr. Lambert surveyed the empty auditorium. The small room had a seating capacity of thirty. It was designed as a place to conduct staff briefings and press conferences. However, because Lambert's staff numbered only six, and they had never accomplished anything especially press-worthy, the place had never been filled. If this afternoon's demonstration was successful, Lambert was sure that the room would soon be too small to contain all of the government officials, and their security details, who would surely be clamoring to meet him.

Along with the accolades heaped upon him, research funding and exclusive contracts would also undoubtedly come his way. He had already made plans to spend his first million. Trips to the south of France. Beautiful women in string bikinis. The second million would buy the beach house and a convertible. Maybe he would even use his new-found popularity to realize a life long fantasy: start a singing career.

Lambert cleared his throat and began to sing. "Mary had a little lamb. Its fleece was white as snow. And everywhere that Mary went, the lamb was sure to go."

The short stocky man standing next to him sighed and shook his head. The two men exited the room. Lambert used a key to lock the door from the outside.

"Okay, now the fun begins," Lambert said to the fat man. "Let's go get some lunch."

2:00 PM

Three men sat in the front row of the auditorium. One was Lambert's associate. The others were representatives from the National Security Agency. Bob Harmon, the fat man, Director of the Agency's New Technologies Division, and Paul Grossman, the bald one, Chief Engineer, New Technologies Division.

Dr. Lambert entered, pulling a wheeled cart, on top of which sat a laptop computer, a portable projector, and some other piece of electronic equipment that the NSA agents could not identify.

"Good afternoon, gentlemen," Dr. Lambert began. As he spoke, Lambert unloaded the equipment from the cart onto a table. He continued speaking as he searched for a file on the laptop and made the proper connections to the projector.

"I'd like to thank you, Mr. Harmon, and Mr. Grossman, for taking the time to come all the way from Maryland to see this demonstration. When I first contacted the NSA over three years ago, I was understandably confronted with skepticism. Thankfully, last year, some of my 'crazy' letters finally reached your desks."

Lambert finished making final connections to his system then addressed his guests directly. "Mr. Harmon, you asked that I contact you again when we had a working prototype. Well, here it is." Lambert's eyes brightened as he waved his hands, Vanna White-like, over the object. The men did not respond.

"Okay," Lambert continued, "before I start the demonstration, I'd like to explain the theory behind the equipment." He pressed a button on the wall behind him. The room lights dimmed and a white screen lowered from the ceiling. Lambert used a handheld remote to control a slide show on the laptop.

The first image projected onto the screen was Vincent Van Gogh's Starry Night.

He began the presentation in the best movie trailer announcer voice he could muster. "From the beginning of recorded history, man has marveled at the beauty of the night sky. But not until recent centuries have we known that, when we look at the stars, we are actually looking back in time."

Lambert pressed a button on the remote control. On the screen, a photograph of the night sky and hundreds of stars replaced the painting. White lines connected dots to form a constellation.

"The closest star to earth, after our sun of course, is Proxima Centauri. It's part of the three-star system that makes up Alpha Centauri. Seen here in the Southern Cross constellation, Proxima Centauri and its sisters are a little over four light years away from us. In other words, it takes four years for the light of that star to travel to us. When we look into the sky, we do not see these stars as they *are*. We see them as they *were*. Four years ago. We are looking at the past!"

He paused and looked at his audience. "So, if we can see the past, can we also hear it?" No response. "Of course we can," he answered his own question.

The Southern Cross was replaced with an illustration of a lone figure standing in a cave. Curved lines representing sound waves radiated from the cave walls.

Lambert cleared his throat and continued the presentation. "When we hear the past, it's called an echo. Stand inside a large cave and yell. Shortly thereafter, you hear the past you calling out. Again . . . and again . . . and again. Although the volume decreases with each iteration, the sound is still there.

"If we can retrieve unheard echoes, we can essentially listen to the past. That's the simple theory on which we based our device. We call the process, Echo Detection and Isolation through Sonic Obstruction Neutralization. 'EDISON,' for short."

The room lights brightened.

"The walls in this room are more or less hard and smooth. Good for reflecting sound waves. The sound waves in this room will bounce around for hours all the while loosing energy and amplitude. Our human ears can't hear the echoes. But they are still there.

"The question is, 'How do we retrieve these echoes?' The answer is simple. You cancel the existing dominant waves and then amplify the underlying echoes. The amount of cancellation will determine how far back in time we hear.

"The construction of some rooms, say, if you have acoustic tiles or noisy air vents, will prevent the Edison device from listening beyond a few minutes into the past. This room, however; will let us go as far back as four hours. I believe that with the further refinements we will be making over the next few years, hopefully with the help of NSA contributions, we will get to the point of listening three to four days into the past in a room like this.

"Okay, enough of me talking. Let's listen to me singing." Lambert smiled. He amused himself often with what he thought were clever witticisms. No one else in the room today seemed to appreciate his humor. "Is this thing on?" He let out a nervous laugh and then took a deep breath. "Okay."

Lambert turned a knob on the EDISON. The device emitted an ear-piercing whistle, momentarily startling the guests. A red light atop the EDISON blinked intermittently. The EDISON sounded musical tones up and down an octave. The flashing light glowed steadily and the room began to grow silent. First, the hum of the ventilation system fell to a whisper and then disappeared. Next, the fan spinning in the projector became inaudible.

Harmon grinned. He shifted his weight in his seat in an attempt to get a better look at the device. Surprisingly, the squeaking of the auditorium chair that accompanied his initial seating was no longer present. Harmon raised an eyebrow and scratched his head. Still no sound.

The red light atop the Edison device changed color to green. The room was completely silent. The NSA guests squirmed uncomfortably as their ears adjusted to the change in air pressure created by the lack of any sound waves pressing on their eardrums.

Lambert adjusted a dial. The green light began to flash. He pressed a button. The light flashed quicker. He turned another dial and pressed the button once more. The green light flashed in sequence with the only sound that filled the room. It was Dr. Lambert's voice. But, the doctor was not speaking. The sound came from the box.

"Mary had a little lamb. Its fleece was white as snow. And everywhere that Mary went, the lamb was sure to go."

4:00 PM

The fat man and the bald one sat across from Dr. Lambert in his office. Lambert rocked slowly in his chair, a nervous habit that he was well aware of. He stopped rocking and asked, "Well, as you can see, we have a working prototype. Is there any way that I, I mean we, can secure NSA funding to further the development?"

Grossman spoke first. "Your device is impressive. It is rather large though. It would be difficult for us to make use of something of that size."

Lambert responded, "Hopefully, with enough developmental money, I will be able to miniaturize the components to a portable size."

Harmon lifted his briefcase and placed it atop Lambert's desk. "We would need something about this size for it to be of any use to us."

Lambert examined the briefcase. It appeared to be maybe seventeen by twelve inches on the face and probably about four inches thick. He thought that he would be able to shrink the EDISON to that size within thirty months. The development would not come cheap. Possibly another eighty million would be needed.

"Yes, I can shrink the EDISON to that size," Lambert said, still gazing down at the briefcase. He took a deep breath, leaned back in his chair, and looked at Harmon. "It'll probably take another four years and around one hundred sixty million dollars." He paused, waiting for a reaction.

The feds remained expressionless.

Lambert turned to the engineer and continued talking. "I know this may sound like a large amount of money but . . . I'm sure you can imagine how valuable an asset the EDISON can be for an information gathering agency such as the NSA."

The engineer looked at Harmon. The two shared a smile. It was the first expression of any type of emotion Lambert had noticed from the duo. Grossman turned to Lambert.

Grossman said, "We have a different proposition for you, Dr. Lambert."

Harmon spoke. "You and your staff will become employees of the National Security Agency."

Grossman continued the thought. "You will all be nicely compensated with a GS-13 salary and receive a full health and dental benefits package."

Lambert sat silently. The words he heard coming out of the mouths of the fat man and the bald one did not make any sense to him. *Work for NSA? GS-13! What kind of fool do these idiots think I am?*

Harmon spoke again. "Your lab will be fully funded to work on cutting-edge projects with national security implications."

Lambert's eyes narrowed. He shifted his gaze from the fat man onto the bald man and back again. *Get the hell out of my office!* No, he couldn't say that. He cleared his throat before beginning to speak. He took a deep breath and began. "Well, gentlemen, that is a kind offer . . . benefits, funded lab . . . interesting. But, in all honesty, I would prefer to remain independent. I'm not looking for a salary. Just operating capital to complete development."

As he spoke, Lambert thought about the other interested parties who had scheduled time for a demonstration. The North Koreans would be here next week. The Chinese the week after that. Either one would easily offer $500 million or more.

Lambert stood and extended a hand across his desk in Harmon's direction. "Thank you again for taking time to come visit us. I will continue to give you progress updates of course, but I'll have to decline your offer."

Neither of the men across the desk moved.

"Please sit down Dr. Lambert," Harmon said. "I think you may have misunderstood us. The salary, the benefits, the funding. They're not an *offer*. They are the terms of your continued operation."

Lambert sat. Confusion and disbelief were evident on his face.

Harmon's voice was low and calm. "In the interest of national security, we can not let you proceed with your research. I'm sure that you can understand the security risk the EDISON would pose, were it to get into the hands of enemies of this country."

"Just think about the information a foreign diplomat could acquire if he carries a portable version of a device like yours into a meeting inside, say, the Oval Office."

"I understand your concerns," Lambert interjected. "But, you can't possibly believe that I would consider selling my technology to anyone who would do harm to the good old U. S. of A."

Grossman answered. "Well, Dr. Lambert, there is something I would like for you to consider." As he spoke, Grossman opened Harmon's briefcase. "First, I want to thank you for giving Mr. Harmon and me some time alone here in your office to discuss things."

Inside the briefcase was a laptop computer. Grossman placed the computer on the desk, opened the lid, and waited for the screen to brighten. He typed hurriedly on the keyboard, from time to time looking up to peer at Lambert.

"This conversation took place here in this office at about 0800 hours today." Grossman pressed *Enter* and the laptop's speakers came to life.

"The NSA people will be here today around eleven. They probably won't be willing to cough up as much as our foreign guys. But I still prefer to do business with them. The transaction will be much easier."

"Definitely. We would have to jump through a lot of hoops to hide the origins of that much foreign cash. We should probably just take what we can get from Uncle Sam.

"But, you know what? If the NSA is not willing to play ball, I'm ready to negotiate with the highest bidder! I've got my eye on a 911 turbo and summer is almost here!"

The voices from the laptop's speakers laughed loudly. Grossman pressed a button and the computer was silent.

Lambert sat expressionless. The blood had flushed from his face. His mind raced to find something to say. "You bugged my office?"

"No, Dr. Lambert," Harmon said. "We're the NSA. Bugs are a thing of the past. Who needs to plant a bug when we can get all the information we want simply by walking into a room?"

Harmon shifted in his chair. "You see, I've followed the development of EDISON out of curiosity. We actually have no need for your device. We made one fifteen years ago."

Harmon waved his hand over the laptop. "And now it works quite well, as you can see. It took a team of thirty to build our device. You guys did yours with only six. I am impressed. Unfortunately, we can't let you profit from your invention. It would put the nation at too great of a risk."

Lambert clinched his fists under his desk. His head was hurting.

"So, you see, our offer to you and your team stands. Come work for us on some cutting-edge projects and enjoy the thrill of working to better your country. Unfortunately, there is no other option. Our friends at Quantico and Langley have made it clear that they will not allow the EDISON, or any information about that device, to leave this country under any circumstances."

Lambert knew who the fat man's friends were and what they were willing to do. The FBI will be watching him and the CIA will be keeping an eye on all of his potential foreign clients. There would be no way that he would be able to sell EDISON. And if he tried, he would probably end up on a missing persons poster.

Lambert asked sheepishly, "What about my Porsche?"

Harmon laughed. "Give us twenty good years and maybe you'll be able to save enough to get that 911."

The two men stood. "Let your staff know the situation. We'll be in touch soon."

They sang as they exited Dr. Lambert's office. "Mary had a little lamb. Its fleece was white as snow."

Touching Things

Allison Garrett greeted the tall, well-dressed man at her front door. Alfred Bell flashed his press credentials. He did not bother to extend a hand to shake. To his knowledge, Garrett had never been clinically diagnosed with any formal anxiety disorder. However, it was well-known that she was somewhat eccentric. She rarely made public appearances, only the occasional literary conference or awards ceremony. When she made those appearances, she generally avoided all forms of personal contact.

Bell was rather surprised when Garrett offered a delicate pale hand. He tentatively extended his hand. He then remembered that the two had indeed shaken hands during their first meeting nearly three years ago. Garrett gripped firmly. They shook for what Bell felt was an uncomfortably long time. She waved the man inside with a smile.

Bell scanned the pristine residence as his hostess led him into the living room. The home was a study of cleanliness and order. The smell of disinfectant lingered in the air. A large floor-to-ceiling window opposite the entry allowed natural light to flood the interior. Garrett's decorating style leaned towards minimalism. The room contained a loveseat, a chaise lounge, a coffee table between the two, a floor lamp, and a small end table next to the chaise. Bell imagined that the area could accommodate two guests at the most. That is, if the author ever entertained guest.

The walls were painted a pure white, which amplified the incoming daylight, giving the area the impression of a large sterile operating room. The only decorations on the walls were a round white clock mounted behind the loveseat and Garrett's framed undergraduate degree beneath the clock. Bell thought it odd that she chose not to display her graduate degrees or the slew of prestigious literary awards she had garnered in her twenty-two year career.

Garrett led her guest to the loveseat. She reclined on the chaise.

"Thank you for having me over," Bell said. "I'm spending a few days of rest and relaxation in your lovely town. I'm glad you were able to take some time and see me."

Garrett smiled and nodded. Bell placed his briefcase on the floor. He pulled a pen and a small notepad from the inside pocket of his jacket.

"I don't know if you remember me. We met once, a few years ago, at a literary event in Chicago."

"Yes. I remember. You have a very distinctive handshake."

Bell's brow wrinkled in confusion. "Ok." He shifted his weight in the chair and continued speaking. "Well, as I mentioned in our phone conversations, I'd like to talk about your new novel, Whisper Loudly, and the inspiration for the serial killer you dreamed up as the antagonist."

"Great," Garrett smiled again. "Before we get started, how about a cup of tea? I've already boiled the water."

"Sure."

Garrett left the room and returned a few minutes later carrying a serving tray loaded with a steaming tea kettle and two cups. She placed the tray on the table, filled the cups, and placed one in front of the reporter and the other on her side of the table.

"Oh, I'm sorry," Garrett exclaimed. "I forgot the sugar and honey. Pardon me, please."

She again exited the room, returning moments later with a small sugar container and a bottle of honey. As she sat, Garrett noticed that Bell's briefcase had been moved. Her cordial smile vanished.

"What's in the briefcase?"

"What? What do you mean?"

"Open it!"

"It's just some research I'm doing on a different story."

Garrett reached for a wooden box sitting on the end table. Bell recognized the box. He had one himself. In his home, the box held the multiple remote controls needed to operate his expansive home entertainment system. Giving the room a quick glance, Bell noticed that there was no electronic equipment in this room.

Garrett opened the box and pulled out a handgun. Pointing the weapon at Bell, Garrett ordered once more, "Open the damn briefcase! Now!"

Bell complied. Setting the briefcase on his lap, he released the dual latches and slowly opened the top. The sound of the gunshot startled him. The .38 caliber round plowed into his right shoulder throwing the reporter back into his seat. The briefcase fell to the floor scattering its contents. The second round hit Bell high in the chest. The bullet ripped through his aorta before lodging in his spine. Bell, partially paralyzed, slumped in the chair as blood and life drained from his body.

Garrett lifted her teacup and drank deeply. The cup was nearly empty after two large sips. She began to feel lightheaded. Garrett went limp in the chaise. She was unconscious within minutes. The gun fell from her hand onto the floor.

****

Garrett awoke in a hospital room. A nurse and doctor hovered nearby. Two police officers stood guard at the doorway. A short stocky man entered the room. He flashed a badge at the doctor and asked, "Is she ok to talk?" The doctor nodded his approval.

"Hello, Ms. Garrett. I'm Detective Jordan. Glad to see you're awake. Do you remember what happened to you?"

Garrett mumbled, "It's not really clear right now."

"That's to be expected. You were drugged. Everything will probably come back to you later." Detective Jordan pulled a chair alongside the bed and sat. "What do you know about the man who came to your home?"

"Um, he's a reporter.

"*Was.*"

"What?"

"He *was* a reporter. Currently, he *is* toe tag number 1220 at the city morgue."

"Oh. I'm sorry."

"No. You shouldn't be. Continue."

"I met him about three years ago at a fundraising event. We hadn't spoken since that night. He contacted me a few weeks ago. He said he wanted to interview me about my new novel."

"Oh yes! Whisper Loudly. That is one very good piece of crime fiction by the way! Well, it looks like he was a huge fan of your book. Maybe your biggest fan of all. He was carrying surgical clamps and scalpels, rope, salt, and sandpaper in his briefcase. Those are the tools your serial killer used, right?"

"Yes," Garrett said.

The detective continued, "We think he planned on torturing and killing you in the same way your guy did his victims in the book. He spiked your drink so he could have his way with you. Apparently, you just got to him first. Lucky you."

Jordan took a deep breath. The images Garrett painted in her best-selling novel were nothing like what he had seen personally in his thirty years of working the occasional homicide in the small town. Her imaginary killer was brutal, yet methodical. Not satisfied with simply incapacitating and dispatching his victims, The Doctor, as he was known in the novel, took a perverse pleasure in cutting, stitching, salting, and taping. The Doctor kept his victims in agony for hours, sometimes days. The thought of someone committing these heinous acts in reality made Jordan shudder.

"I think we can clear this one up quickly. I just have a couple of questions for you." The detective pulled a pen and notepad from the inside pocket of his jacket. "Where do you keep your gun and how did you manage to reach it before Mr. Bell started working on you?"

"Well," Garrett cleared her throat, "um, I'm a bit overly cautious, if you're not aware. I have two guns in my home. Both are registered, of course. I keep one in the night table beside my bed and the other in a box in the living room."

Jordan jotted on the notepad. "Are they under lock and key?"

"No. I know that's not really safe, but. They're for my protection. I don't live with anyone and I don't generally entertain guests. So, there's no chance of someone accidentally finding them."

Garrett shifted uncomfortably in the bed. "I remember feeling dizzy and seeing him pull a knife out of his briefcase. I reached for my gun. But . . . that's all I remember."

Detective Jordan stood and extended a hand to shake. Garrett tentatively reached out. As their skin made contact, Garrett's mind flooded with memories flowing from the detective. Garrett experienced these memories as if they were her own. She saw herself at eight years old attending funeral services for her slain police officer father. She saw herself graduating the police academy twelve years later. She remembered paying off rival gang members to murder each other with a promise of immunity.

The detective pulled his hand back after what he felt was an uncomfortably long time. "You're a lucky woman." He smiled. "Just by looking at someone, you never know what kind of freak that person may be."

"Yes. You're right, detective." Garrett returned the detective's pensive smile with one of her own. "You never know . . . just by looking. Thank you."

"I may need to talk to you again later. Get some rest now."

"Ok."

Garrett continued smiling as Detective Jordan exited. She knew that she had found the subject of her next best-selling crime novel. She would need to be more diligent in changing some of the details this time.

Alfred Bell, The Doctor, was the first of her subjects to recognize himself in her work. She had gotten lazy. That wouldn't happen again.

Garrett called out to a passing nurse, "Nurse, will you please see if you can find me a pair of gloves?" She grimaced, clasped her hands together and pulled them to her chest. "I really don't like touching things with my bare hands."

How DVDs Saved My Life

It started about a year ago. Actually, I'm not sure when it really started. Let's just say that I first *became aware of it* about a year ago. That's when the picture on my favorite big screen television, the one that I'd had for less than two years, began to dim and distort. The picture did not disappear, but the quality was far from the 1080i high definition picture for which I had paid so dearly.

Let me just say right now that I love watching my television. I watch at least five hours of broadcast or satellite television a day. I have also collected the DVD box sets of my favorite television series and have watched every season . . . multiple times . . . and then watched them again, while listening to the directors' and actors' commentaries. My movie collection is massive too. I have every movie on all of the "Best Of" lists for every genre. I maintain a weekly online blog with reviews, comments, and criticisms of plots, characters, and production value. So, there. You know my background. In short, I am a TV/DVD junkie.

Of course, a junkie can't live long without a fix. So, after a few weeks of watching disfigured images, I replaced the faulty television with a brand new 1080p model. The new television gave me months of enjoyment. But, within weeks of buying the television, my laptop computer began malfunctioning and shutting down automatically. Ok. Yes, I am also an Internet addict. Nothing can be better than sitting in front of my 1080i, well, now 1080p, watching a movie while simultaneously googling its stars, or IMDB-ing the title to add some trivia that these other so-called movie buffs have no clue about! So, without hesitation, I bought a new computer to replace my dying one.

At first, my damaged electronics didn't cause me much concern. Frustration? Yes, but not concern. I figured it was just coincidence that two of my favorite machines would break down at roughly the same time. I thought it was just coincidence, until a neighbor a few blocks down the road had the exact same problems. Television blinking, computer won't boot. That's when I got suspicious. However, what confirmed my suspicions was the news that a secret U.S. government spy satellite had lost power and was beginning to fall to earth.

You see, the aliens in *Independence Day,* the 1996 summer blockbuster derivative of H.G. Wells' classic, The War of the Worlds, initiated their invasion by taking over our communications satellites. Of course, in the movie, the aliens used the satellites to synchronize a global attack. That didn't seem to be the case here. But, if you think about it, it's obvious now that the combination of events I have described was the precursor of an alien invasion. The malfunctioning electronics and the dead satellite were tests. The aliens needed to prove that were really able to shut down all of our electronics. You are following the logic, aren't you?

On the night of February 3rd, I found out why the alien tests were so important. There was a blackout that night in Jersey City, NJ. It happened about thirty minutes after the end of the Super Bowl.

If you remember from *Close Encounters of the Third Kind*, a blackout heralded the aliens' arrival. So, the Jersey City blackout confirmed my conclusions. I knew they were coming. But, unlike the big-headed greys of

Close Encounters, these aliens were not coming to make friends. They wanted something from us. They wanted *us*.

In the three hours that the lights were out in downtown Jersey City, a small group of people looted the Newport City Mall. The mob smashed windows and grabbed clothing and jewelry. Sane human beings would never act that way. What I determined was that these were not human beings at all. Sure, their outer bodies were human, but inside, they were being controlled, or possessed, I'm not sure what to call it. Inside, they were undoubtedly inhabited by aliens.

I know how the aliens accomplished this. If you take a look at *Invasion of the Body Snatchers* (either the 1956 version or the 1978 version) you will see that alien invaders can't enter a human host easily. I commend Jack Finney, the author of the novel on which the movies were based, for realizing how difficult it is to possess a human being. In the novel, and both versions of the movie, aliens were only able to replace a person when that person was asleep.

Unlike *Invasion of the Body Snatchers*, the aliens that invaded Jersey City could indeed enter people during their waking hours. But the aliens could only do it during a blackout. At the time, I wondered why. But, after some deep thinking, it's all so apparent now!

The background electrical interference caused by our modern power grid and home electronics makes it difficult for the aliens to enter our bodies. The megavolts of power carried along the country's power lines create invisible electromagnetic energy fields. Even when the power is stepped down to levels that can safely power our home appliances, the fields exist. As a matter of fact, our televisions, computers, microwave ovens, refrigerators, vacuum cleaners, and all of our other appliances that we plug into our homes' outlets add to the cacophony of electromagnetic noise all around us. For some reason, which I haven't quite yet surmised, this electrical interference must prevent the alien entities from possessing human bodies.

So, there. I put all of the pieces of the puzzle together. Jersey City was the first wave of the invasion. The aliens produced a blackout, thereby disabling the power grid and all of the electronics in the city. With the man-made electromagnetic interference gone, their troops easily took over as many bodies as they could, and in a crazed frenzy, looted the mall. Simple yet brilliant!

After I was aware of their secret, I took steps to ensure that I would never become one of their puppets. I went to the home supply store and purchased a top-of-the-line 45kW liquid-cooled generator to tie into my home electrical network. I paid over $14,000, but that's a small price to pay for my life. I am ready for the next blackout. I will never be without power. I will never be possessed.

I work from home now. My groceries are delivered to my door, and anything that I need can be ordered from the internet. I have created a fortress with walls of impenetrable electromagnetic energy.

I believe that the aliens will wait until summertime to begin the real invasion. During the summer, they will be able to cause blackouts without raising any suspicions. Thunderstorms and excessive air conditioning usage are blamed for overloading the power grid and causing blackouts all the time. The aliens will use these events to mask the blackouts that they produce this summer, and begin their invasion one community at a time. They will have to be patient. It will probably take years to infect everyone.

As for me, I will be safe here at home, running my generator and watching my DVDs. I can't tell anyone what I know about the invasion. They will think that I am crazy, and would likely try to remove me from my fortress. Do you remember *Invasion of the Body Snatchers* (1956), the version with the prologue and epilogue, not the shorter version that was released later? Remember how Dr. Bennell was being treated in the beginning? They were ready to escort the doctor off to an insane asylum as they listened non-believingly to his story!

I refuse to be treated like Dr. Bennell. No. I will not tell anyone what I know. I'm going to wait it out. If I've learned anything from my DVDs, I know that hostile alien invasions will eventually be fought off and human life will go on. For example, in *War of the Worlds* (2005), the aliens brought civilization to the brink of destruction, only to be conquered by the earth's smallest creatures – viruses. In *Independence Day* a virus defeated those aliens there too, only in that adaptation, it was a computer virus.

The battle will rage on outside, but I will be safe inside. My next objective is to figure out how to develop some form of electrical virus capable of killing the invading army. It may take years to complete. And I'll probably have to end all contact with my family and friends because who knows how long they'll remain uninfected. But that's ok. I won't get bored or lonely. I have my DVDs to keep me entertained.

Secret Vacations, Inc.

Your Boss Won't Know That You're Away!

Ron Hamilton read the subject line of the email again. The message had appeared in his office inbox a few minutes earlier. There was no indication of who the sender was. On any other day, Ron would have assumed that this was just more junk mail and would have deleted the message without a second thought. But, this was not any other day. This was a Friday at the end of a week in which Ron's concentration and motivation to work had gradually faded to nearly nothing. Today at the office, he had put in equal amounts of time fantasizing about piña coladas on pink sand beaches and searching the Internet for the price of run-flat tires for his Boxster.

He opened the message.

Mr. Hamilton:

Please do not delete this email. My name is Dr. Cyrus Angelo. My group operates Secret Vacations, Inc. Our company offers unique vacation opportunities for a select clientele. Imagine getting away from the office for a full week without anyone even knowing that you've been gone! That's what we can do for you.

Secret Vacations, Inc. has been in operation for over two years now with 100% customer satisfaction. We currently have eighty members in your city. Our services are unique and discrete. Because of our business model, we will only be able to open our doors to one hundred customers in each of America's fifty most populous cities. Due to your income and past travel history, you have been identified as a one of those potential one hundred in this market.

Unfortunately, I am unable to discuss the specifics of our operation in this email. If it appears that our services would appeal to you, please meet me at our corporate offices, 927 September Avenue NW, at 5:30 PM this afternoon.

Thank you for your time. I hope to see you today.

Best Regards,

Dr. Cyrus Angelo, PhD.
CEO, Secret Vacations, Inc.

Ron closed the email. He looked at his watch. It was already a quarter after four. He could easily leave the office at five o'clock and walk to September Ave. The address was only five blocks away. He decided that that was what he would do. This would be a fitting end to the week.

Ron had started the week with an intense concentration that he had never remembered having before. Monday, he had thought, was the most productive day of his career. He made significant progress on two projects over which he had spent months procrastinating. However, as the week progressed, his focus diminished.

On Tuesday, the first thoughts of vacationing popped into his head. Out of curiosity, he had spent an hour surfing the Internet, searching for last minute vacation deals. Wednesday and Thursday were more of the same. He figured he had probably wasted two or three hours on each of those days searching for a getaway bargain. Actually, he didn't really waste those hours. His searching had paid off. He found a couple of reasonably priced packages. One week in Bermuda. Five days in the Cayman Islands. He bookmarked the sites and tried to return his attention to his work.

Today was the worst day of the week. It started with an extra push of his alarm clock's snooze button. Nine more minutes of sleep. Ron had absolutely no desire to come into the office this morning so he delayed getting out of the bed as long as he could. Usually, he would press the snooze button only once. Today, he pressed it twice. Nine more minutes in the bed. Who would have thought that nine minutes would make such a big difference in the course of a day?

He left his house at 6:54 AM, instead of 6:45 AM. The commute from his suburban Maryland home into downtown Washington, DC was usually a predictable forty-five minute drive. He'd leave his neighborhood, head north on MD210, hop onto I-295 North, and ride straight into the city.

This morning, a toolbox fell from the back of a pickup truck a few minutes into his commute on I-295. In what appeared to Ron as a slow-motion video clip, the red chest tumbled onto the highway. After bouncing on the pavement twice, the latch opened and spilled its contents of workman's tool onto the street. A wrench skipped to the left of Ron's car.

A pair of screwdrivers danced their way past the right side. He saw the claw hammer somersaulting directly towards the front of his car. There was no time to swerve. The slow motion movie switched speeds to fast forward. In the blink of an eye, his car was rolling over the hammer. He felt the *thump-thump* of front and rear tires rolling over the tool.

When he parked his car at the office, Ron inspected the tires. The front driver's side tire had a gash in the tread. He could hear air seeping through the crack.

* * * * *

Ron Hamilton logged out of his computer at 5:20 PM. He packed a briefcase with folders and loose papers. The guilt of goofing off all day weighed on his conscious. He thought that maybe he would pull the work out over the weekend and

complete the tasks that he had neglected today. He left the office nine minutes early and began the short walk to the address in the strange email.

927 September Avenue NW, the address of Secret Vacations, Inc. The building was a modest nineteenth century row house converted into office space. The brown brick façade looked oddly out of place on this street occupied by sleek glass and steel-framed twenty-first century office buildings.

While neighborhoods such as Dupont Circle and Georgetown contain an aesthetically pleasing mix of old and new, the city's urban renewal plans of the 1970's subjected the long-neglected September Avenue to an almost complete razing. The century-old row house, now the home of a business copy center, a real estate agency, and a travel agency, was the only building deemed worthy of salvaging on a four-block stretch of the street. The Secret Vacations, Inc. offices occupied the third floor of the row house.

* * * * *

Hamilton sat across a desk from Dr. Cyrus Angelo. He did not look at the doctor. Instead, he stared out of the window behind the doctor. The large bay window behind Dr. Angelo offered a panoramic view of the city. From this vantage point, Hamilton remembered how beautiful he thought Washington really was. In his hectic work-a-day existence, he had neglected to appreciate even little thing like this.

"Mr. Hamilton," Angelo began, "I want to thank you for coming to see us. I'm sorry about the cryptic invitation, but once you understand what we have to offer, you'll know why we have to take certain . . . precautions when approaching potential clients."

"Sure," Hamilton responded, bringing his thoughts under control and focusing attention on his host. "I was a little suspicious of your email. It looked like some crazy spam scam. But, it came at the right time. I'm in serious need of a vacation. I've never heard of your travel agency. But since you're right down the street from my office, I figured I would stop by and see what you have to offer."

Angelo smiled. He took in a deep breath, paused, and began speaking slowly. "Mr. Hamilton, we're more than just a travel agency. We're a full-service *entertainment and life management agency.*"

Hamilton's brow furrowed in confusion. "Excuse me?"

"This company is like no other travel agency that you have ever heard of. Yes, if you want to book a trip to Tahiti, we can do that for you, no problem. For our preferred clients, which we hope you will become, we offer much more than a travel package.

"The email I sent you earlier today. The message heading was 'your boss won't know that you are away' correct?"

Hamilton nodded.

Angelo continued. "What if I told you that wasn't just an attention-getter? What if I told you that my company can arrange your dream vacation and ensure that life goes on, here at home, just as if you never left?"

"How can you do that?"

"We have a technology that makes it all possible. You'll have to understand though that this is proprietary information. If you are interested in taking advantage of our preferred services, I will insist that you sign our non-disclosure agreement before we continue."

"Sure, whatever."

Angelo reached into a desk drawer and retrieved a stack of papers. He slid the papers, along with a pen, across the desktop to Hamilton.

"Please. Take as much time as you need to read the documents. If you agree, please initial and sign at the bottom of each page in the space provided."

Hamilton studied the top page of the stack. His name, address, and personal contact telephone numbers were already typed in a section labeled *client information.* Hamilton thumbed through the remaining pages. He counted sixteen in all. He returned to the first page and initialed and signed in the space provided at the bottom.

"Please, Mr. Hamilton, take your time and read."

"No need. I want to hear what you have to offer. I'm not telling anyone." Hamilton initialed and signed the remaining pages. "Let's get started." He slid the stack across the desk to Angelo.

Angelo gathered the papers and placed them in a manila folder. "What do you know about tissue cloning, neural mapping, and advanced robotics?" he asked.

The question was rhetorical. Angelo had done his research. He knew that Hamilton, an avid science buff and amateur inventor, had a general knowledge of many of the latest medical and scientific breakthroughs. However, what Angelo was about to tell Hamilton would sound more like science fiction than science fact to the man.

Angelo continued, "Forget what you *think* you know. The reality of what's going on in laboratories around the globe is light years more advanced."

Hamilton slid his body nearer the front of his chair and leaned in closer to the doctor.

"This company, Secret Vacations, is a wholly-owned subsidiary of Cheetah Werks Corporation. Are you familiar with Cheetah Werks?" This time, Angelo's question was not rhetorical. He paused to give his guest time to reply.

Hamilton nodded, acknowledging his familiarity with the organization. Cheetah Werks was a very well-financed research and development think tank whose emphasis was on advanced technologies. The Company lured the world's top scientists with very lucrative short term contracts to work on its major projects. Cheetah Werks made the bulk of its money from the sale of licensing rights for patents it held in the areas of microelectronics and biomedical engineering.

Cheetah Werks' most recent news-worthy announcement was its claim that it was within ten years of perfecting what it called the Ultra-Wideband Direct Neuro Communicator. In essence, the device would be a cell phone with a direct connection to the brain. The group claimed that users of the UWB DNC would be able to initiate conversations with one another simply by *thinking* of a phone number or unique contact code. Once connected, the two parties would communicate non-verbally, their thoughts converted to words or images and transmitted directly into each others' minds. Mind reading made a reality, through technology.

What Ron did not know was that Cheetah Werks was also surreptitiously under contract with the United States Department of Defense to develop new weapons technology for the battlefield. The UWB DNC would certainly find its way into soldiers' brains. But the company had an even more radical plan in mind for the nation's military.

"So why would the world's leading tech firm have an interest in running a travel agency?" Hamilton asked.

"Cheetah Werks has quite a few projects underway in various stages of development. Sometimes we need to conduct real world beta testing in order to iron out the kinks. This travel agency is just one of many businesses used for that purpose."

"I don't understand. So, what, you're saying that this is just some kind of a fund raising front for CW?" Hamilton's voice began shaking, revealing his sudden agitation. "Are you going to try to sell me a timeshare in some kind of a high tech 'smart' condo in Seattle now?"

Dr. Angelo raised his palms to Hamilton and patted the air in a calming motion.

"No, no, no, this isn't a sales pitch." The tone of the doctor's voice switched from conversational to business-like. "I want to tell you about Cheetah Werks' Synthetic Human project. Secret Vacations is field testing the first generation line."

"What's that?"

"It's the convergence of several ongoing research projects. The goal is to create a precise replica of a human being. We use our robotics division to build an articulated humanoid skeleton, brain scanning capacity to map human thought processes onto a portable CPU, and tissue cloning to cover the whole gizmo in real human skin. Add a power source and, abracadabra, you have an artificial human that moves, thinks, and feels exactly like the living, breathing person it was modeled after.

"We're offering 100 lucky people the opportunity to take a break from their hectic lives and let a Synthetic Human step into their shoes for a week."

"How much does this service cost?"

"It costs you absolutely nothing. We simply ask that our customers leave town during the week of the test. Unless you have an identical twin brother, we can't risk reports of seeing you in two places at the same time." Angelo chuckled.

"So that's what you meant by *your boss won't know you're away*?"

Over the next hour, Angelo explained how the process would work. A few skin cells would be taken from Hamilton and cultured in a laboratory. It would take a month to grow enough skin to cover the Synthetic Human's face and hands. Hamilton's brain would be scanned. Selected memories and his general thought process would be mapped onto an artificial brain. Finally, the skin and brain would be merged with a robotic skeleton to produce a synthetic Ron Hamilton.

Although his mind had wandered at times during the doctor's presentation, Hamilton liked what he heard.

* * * * *

Ron Hamilton arrived at work early on the following Monday morning. He was feeling excited to be back in the office.

He sifted through papers and post-it notes strewn about his desk trying to determine which of his projects needed his attention this week.

Ron's desk phone rang. He smiled when he read the name on the caller id. Secret Vacations. Ron raised the receiver and answered the call with a hearty, "Good morning, Dr. Angelo!"

"Good morning, Mr. Hamilton," the voice on the other end of the line replied. "I take it that you enjoyed your week off? No complaints?"

"Well, I'm looking over the work that my Synthetic did last week. So far, everything looks ok. I haven't spoken to anyone, so I'm not sure how convincing my replacement was just yet.

"I do know that he, or, it had a minor accident with my car. I need a new front tire."

"Not to worry, Mr. Hamilton, we will cover all damages. After all, you are helping us to perfect our product. Please, let us know if you're planning another getaway in the near future. We've found a small processing error in the system. We've made some adjustments and we would like to see how the new programming works."

"Really, what kind of error?"

"Well, it seems that the artificial brain begins to loose its ability to remain on task after three or four days in the field. This results in what appears to be a total lack of concentration. Spells of, what can only be considered as, daydreaming. And generally lolly-gagging about. Luckily, this does not affect the pre-programmed homing instinct. Your model responded to my email and returned to us at precisely five-thirty last Friday afternoon, as your contract stipulated. It had no idea that it was a Synthetic Human. In fact, it expressed interest in using our service." The doctor chuckled. "We talked about Secret Vacations for an hour. At six-thirty, its program shut off and we took it to diagnostics to review its data."

"Anyway," Dr. Angelo continued, "we've made some adjustments to your model and we would like to test them at your earliest convenience. Whenever you're in the mood for another week off, just give us a call."

"Sure. I'll let you know when I'm ready. Thanks for your service. Hopefully I'll see you in a month or two. Have a good day."

"You too, Mr. Hamilton."

Hamilton placed the telephone receiver on its base, turned to his computer, and opened an Internet browser window. A knock at the door interrupted his activity.

The door opened and Kenneth Ramsey's six-foot-three-inch frame filled Hamilton's doorway. "Good morning, Ron. Do you have a minute?" His boss entered the office before Hamilton could answer.

Ramsey set a few papers on Hamilton's desk. Summaries of work that had been completed by Hamilton the previous week. Ramsey expressed his extreme pleasure with the quality of the work.

As his boss spoke, Hamilton wondered if the man in front of him was indeed a man. Was it possible that Kenneth Ramsey was a client of Secret Vacations? Sure. It was possible, Hamilton thought.

The conversation lasted for five minutes. Hamilton waited until his boss exited his office and was several feet down the hallway before turning his attention to his computer screen. The Caribbean is nice this time of year.

Neal McNeil

Neal McNeil has a B.S. in Electrical Engineering from Hampton University. He currently works full time as an engineer in Washington, DC, and part-time as an actor in local film, television, and stage productions. Inspired by classic television series such as The Twilight Zone and The Outer Limits, Mr. McNeil's short stories combine science, humor, and drama producing thought-provoking and compelling entertainment.

Mr. McNeil lives in Maryland with his wife and stepson. He is currently completing his first novel.

Made in the USA